U0114300

博客思出版社

濱海札記
Seashore variegates

散文及十四行詩
Sonnet and Sketches

賴慶曉
Anthony Lai 著

目錄
Catalog

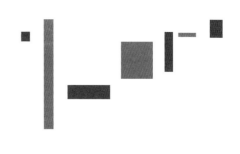

■ 內容介紹

本書由三種元氣混血組成

十四行詩源於義大利,有小詩小歌之意。

初不限十四行後定型為十四行,傳入英國之後,結構改變,分為 3 段四句加最後兩句。最後的兩句通常為反意或合饋。現代則較自由不為行數押韻所限。

俳句源於日本,在第一次戰後漸在歐美流行,古俳有字數季節限制,今俳我較重於意境,不足以成詩的短句。

散文那就是較細節的述陳,比較囉唆的感觸。

用中英對照,其實不盡然對照,用英文描繪的,譯中不盡其意,

用中文為詩,英文也都幾難通釋,中英文,讀者惟自賞之。

Introductions

This book composed by three vitalities of blood.

The sonnets

Sonnet originated in Italy, a poem or song narrating a story in short stanzas.

No limit at the beginning, after stereotypes into fourteen lines.

Later, being introduced to the UK, structural changes.

Divided into 3 paragraphs each in four sentences plus the last two sentences.

The last two sentences are usually antagonistic or co-feeding.

More in modern styles, not limited by the rhyme of the number of lines.

Haiku originated from Japan.

After the first war gradually became popular in Europe and America.

Ancient haiku has the number of characters and seasonal restrictions.

Modern, as I am focused on artistic conception, then the form.

In another meaning, few short sentences which not enough to make of a poem.

Prose is a more detailed statement, a more insulting touch.

The comparison between Chinese and English is actually not a complete comparison. What is described in English is not exactly what it means in translation.

Use Chinese and English, in fact, they are not completely contrasted, and what is described in English is not exactly what it means in Chinese translation.

Chinese poem, English is very difficult to fully express, vice versa, Chinese or English, is readers self-admiration.

作者 序

安德烈 • 紀德，在其早期的著作《地糧》表達一種狀態「愈飲 我愈感口渴。最後這渴念那樣強烈，我竟為欲望痛哭」。

詩是情感狀態的表徵，從內心燒，太久太熾，用手寫在 AI 臉上就成詩。

這本用十四行詩形骸寫的「詩集」夾雜引述用的「散文」、「俳句」共分為三大部份。

Bartok 滿州大人，開始是用舞台劇形式的十四行詩作敘述性的變奏，加上了 Pizza 店老板，無臉男角色，結合有趣唯美的虛，把荒謬的想像，用我敲擊的文字作速描，加了很多圖片，我認為，在看詩的時侯 不那麼冰冷，從而鏡射讀者內心的渴望，愛慾的冥想。

後來，我延申到劇中，那舞女的懷孕，開啟了給一個懷孕女人的詩篇，我的詩中強調，真以及美沒有善，因為那是倫理的範疇。

最後一些十四行詩，就是我私人生活的臉，母親 兒孫們。

一個朋友看了我的詩，她說，我掙扎中享受，在享受中掙扎，或許是。

Preface

Andre Gide expressed a state in his early work *Foods on Ground*, (French: *Les nourritures terrestres*), expressed "The more I drink, the more thirsty I feel. In the end, this longing was so strong that I was crying for".

Poetry is a representation of an emotional state. It is burned from the heart for too long and too hot. Handwritten on the face of the AI becomes a poem.

This collection of poems written in a sonnet frame, mixed with prose and Haiku for narration, is divided into three parts.

Start with the Sonnet, Bartok Manchuria

Use stage-play sonnets to make narrative variations, adding the faceless male character, the Pizza shop owner, combined with imagination pictures, adding absurd thoughts to sketch with the words I knocked on.

There are a lot of pictures and photos, I think it will make you less cold when you are reading poems, so that you can mirror your inner desire for eros meditation.

Later on, I extended that the pregnancy of the dancing girl in the play opened a serious of poem for the pregnant woman.

My poem emphasized truth and beauty without virtuous.

Because that is the category of ethics, I don't hide the place where it happens. If I did, it is not from the touches of my ordinary life.

The last section of sonnets are the face of my private life, mother, children and grandchildren

A friend of mine read my poem and she said I struggle to enjoy, and also enjoy the struggling. Well...maybe.

「散文」則是詩間的串聯比較難用簡潔昇華文字表達。

而「俳句」飯後的咖啡、甜點。

至於，量子、宇宙、星系，如果你不是星際大戰影迷，那把那些東西看成「未具現的」思維即可。

感謝我弟，賴瑞祥醫師，一直支持我出版。

也很感謝博客思，幫我出版這冷門的十四行詩集。

好啦！奈黛奈藹，如今，拋開我這書。使你自己從我的書中解脫出來。離開我！回到你的〈地糧〉吧！

看完了這本詩集，我希望你能燔祭一些你的思維。

賴慶曉

Prose is a connection between poems, which can't be expressed by simple sublimation, but haiku, after a meal, they are coffee and dessert.

As for the quantum universe, galaxy, if you are not a fan of Star Wars, just treat those things as unrealized thinking.

Thanks to my brother Dr. Lai Rui Xiang for supporting me in publishing.

I'm also very grateful to LEARNING TIDE PUBLICATION CO., LTD. for helping me publish this unpopular collection of sonnets.

Alright! Nata Naa, now, put aside my book. Free yourself from my book, leave me! Go back to eat your own ground food!

After reading this book of poems, I hope you can burn some of your thoughts out.

Anthony Lai

大和 日本料理店 對話

那本書,該說「我的這本書」是從什麼人說的,什麼地方開採來的最後變成我的──時間空間礦石。

有如日本料理店,服務生上生魚片,這是師傅,用光秒織成的畫布,作為奉食的。

用手拿著料理盤,沾染上送來時,指隙時光的細粉,留在端來的足印上。

而我用文字,盡量寫在數位的 AI 臉上,印刷、成冊、散發、出版。

不過是,讓某些人知道〈時光〉曾經在我身上彩繪,在我染色體上〈註記〉。

只是使用只有自己才記得的思維中,最細小的記憶量子,加疊成文字。

有光的地方,看見暗黑的地方,我知道,纏結了的她有回想,才知道,把切好的陳鋪在彩盤上的,拉成「多重維元」成某〈宇宙〉。

不能,也不要用現在去修改過去,過去覺得的會寫下,刻上,既然成了文字,己上桌的菜,不能修改。

Yamato Japanese Restaurant Dialogue

The book or say, this book, my book always part from somewhere, someone.

Or from nowhere, no one, but in the end become my time, space, and stones from mind.

As a waitress, she said: "Time have had lived on the brushes moisten tinny sand, stone, caved the linen canvas by stiches and elapsed from the trace I just walked."

I written in the digitized AI face as hard as possible, press, print, published spread.

Just for me or anyone touch the colorful lights on my dying body

修改或許想潤澤文字，不該是改變初始的衷曲。

要丟掉、捨棄的，將來有人會替你做。她說。

用不著你現在做，你只能記下，下一瞬或許即忘不再記起。

本來想從上帝亞伯拉罕，摩利亞山上 PIZZA 店說起 (1)

但那也是催生，冬眠後的產物，算了。

就從那 Bartok 滿大人 (2) 音樂以及序曲，十四行詩的〈裸琴〉

說起。

once before.

My DNA been marked from notes refer to my thought quantum overlapped to.

Tangled her memories when she thinks of me, lighting my face when I am thinking of her.

And hens if I can draw, I will draw as multiple dimensions as a new Universe as paint.

She spoked more, no attempt to change the recorder of your past script, probable retouching.

But never change the original thinking.

Abandoned will be by someone, you can only record, do not betray the pleasant now appeared, because in a second, you will forget.

Talking originally about the Mount Moriah, but it was a past hibernate ecbolic by a plangent woman.

That us beginning in Bartok (The Miraculous Mandarin) and raised by the music of naked Cello.

18
濱海札記

十四行詩 |sonnet

014 裸琴
014 naked Cello

安東尼 · 賴
十四行詩 014

裸　琴

我把妳的　裸照　放大　畫上　五條弦
從鼻尖　到肚臍　的　定位　虛弦
從雙眼下　伸到　雙腿內側的　淋巴結ＧＤ弦
從高漲　奶頭　垂線到　腳指尖ＣＡ弦

我坐在妳　照片　後面　大提琴　頭頸　斜靠著肩
春繪　的　長弓　若然　撫動著　的　弦
我的　指尖　按著　不同的　高低位　譜成音樂
弓弦的　振動　如浪波　迴盪　來自琴腔的　渦漩

壓在 gd線　我們眼中　流出了淚　淹沒　疲憊的知覺
壓在 ca線　生命的　虹彩飛濺　振動光蕪的　歲月
壓住定位虛線　纏卷　沒有音樂　急促喘息　如雷
琴腔無法　共鳴　因愛盈滿　雲雨飛漲

沒有調弦音的琴　有弓
只拉　也空洞的　幻音

Anthony Lai

Sonnet 014

naked Cello

I zoomed in on your nude photo and put five strings on it.
Positioning virtual string from nose tip to belly button.
G D string of lymph nodes extending, under the eyes
to the inside of the legs.
From the vertical line of the rising nipples to the toes, the
C A string.

I'm sitting behind your picture, cello head and neck
leaning on shoulder.
The string bow of spring painted your heart.
My fingertips compose music according to different high
and low positions.
Vibration of the bowstring waves resounds, and the vortex
reverberated.

Pressed on the gd line, tears shed in our eyes, drowning
our tired perceptions.
Pressing on the ca line, the iridescent splash of life,
 vibrating the feeless years.
Squeeze the positioning dotted line, wrap around, no
music, respite like thunder.
The Cello can't resonate because of love, clouds, and rain
soring.

Without tuning, just has a bow.
Only create the hollow phantom sound.

22

濱海札記

十四行詩 | sonnet

滿洲大人 | The Miraculous Mandarin

夜　鶯

離上次　我與亞伯 (1) 上摩利亞山

又是 5000 光年後的冬雪紛飛的夜晚

摩利亞山上的 Pizza 店 (2)　己改成劇院

正上演 Bartok　滿州大人　被　上吊　那一幕

Pizza 店老板　在編劇　轉頭問　來獻祭？

滿大人從鐥曲美伶　懷中

跳下舞台　我要獻祭　Bartok

老板不允許　把他變成一尊石像

Anthony Lai

Sonnet | The Miraculous Mandarin 008

Nightingale

Memory, the path of last sacrifice,[1]
as another windy snowshoer, same place seagoing.
The Pizza Hall[2], now Drama Orchestra, 5000LY, apostle
spray.
Evolve, Bartok, The Miraculous Mandarin[3] , last scene,
Hanging.

Pizza Boss, weaving, hey, for sacrifice alone ?
The Mandarin, jump from tangled woman arms, out of the
stage.
Sacrifice "Bartok", and save me, ... No...
Turn into a status stone.

Sacrifice my Nightingale—for the sake of having no night.
Covered with black canopy, singing eco forbidden songs.
Feed golden cone makes me exhausted.
Smelt by philosopher's stone[4], no longer left in my
quintessence.

Need no more now, the brightness of outside world.
My Nightingale, will fade, as Seagull, hunting fishes.

我要祭我的　夜鶯　我的國度沒有　夜

養成的　關閉籠內　黑布蓋著　騙她　唱歌

用黃金雕飾的　玉米球　喂食

我　提煉黃金　的賢石 (3) 已用罄

那白晝　如此明亮　不需　歌聲佴傳

那似錦如織的　世界　她褪成　海鷗　追逐魚群

Seashore variegates

間　奏

午後　小睡　詭異的單簧管聲　吹起（13:11）
那是個　斷斷續續的　旋律主題
三惡徒　教她如何　搔首弄姿
女子開始首次的誘舞

我卻被瞬移到劇院舞台前
Pizza 店　老板 (1) 打量我　嗯……合適
我沒要燔祭　為何瞬移 (2) 對身體不好耶！
量子與逆旋量子　鏡像而己　又不是實體

Anthony Lai

Sonnet | The Miraculous Mandarin 009

inter perform (Decoy Game)

Noonday nap, (13:11) Clarinet spooky sound, raised
an intermittent melody.
From my back neck,
a needle-like pain, no sting, but teleport.
The scene- three tramps ask her-Saucy dance.

Why? Force teleport? Heart my body.
I have nothing need to sacrifice, not a thing.
He looks me with 'Hum',
Hay, just quantum negative transfer, no big deal.
Oh sorry, your quantum mind could be change.

I have a request , the Pizza Boss speak,
Need your oil paint - Narcissus[1] - sacrifice here.
He needs be part of Bartok, to compensate, The Mandarin,
I lost.
I will give you Promised Land[2] , as your desire.

Knife lift, the Narcissus exist, and I lost.
Hah, embodiment test, let her become a Pregnant Woman,
and you, sacrifice your face for another 5000LY.

可是　我的思維量子　會有變異

那倒是　想借用你的東西　油畫　納西瑟斯 (3) 的臉

拿來燔祭　我答應給你　允諾之地

於是我拿了畫　又瞬移　我舉刀　納西瑟斯　現身

我忘了我是誰

嘿嘿⋯⋯小小試驗　納西瑟斯　誘惑她

成為　（一個懷孕的女人）

而你　無臉男 (4) 借臉 5000 光年

安東尼 · 賴

謝　幕

電梯速度　暗黑　頸背刺麻　我知　又被　瞬移
來到濱海居所　沙崙盡頭　古堡　囚　懷孕女人
巫師迎來　不捨及問　被拉到幕前　在 Pizza 店老板　左位
同　右位　三惡人　無臉男　納西瑟斯　向鏡眾謝幕

鏡眾噪　換檔　愛情故事　美好結局
老板向我攤手　唉！滿檔 5000 光年
沒有棧戀
斜眼　似笑非笑　心知　有兆
允諾之地？老板　面有難色　無言

那堡中囚著一個懷孕女子　舞者？
緣何囚？納西瑟斯　說　她懷了
Bartok 小宇宙 (1)

救贖吧！被瞬移者　不知名者　無身份者
無臉男跪求　納西瑟斯淚崩

Anthony Lai

Sonnet | The Miraculous Mandarin 010

Curtain Call

Dim elevator, stabling spine, noticed been teleportation.
The Castle prison a pregnant woman,
end of the shallow sand residence.
Shaman welcome me, pass by the cell,
direct to left hand side by Pizza Boss.
Together right with three tramps,
Narcissus, and Faceless man, curtain call.

Insurgences ask, happy ending, affection story, no
obscure.
Vulnerable spread, 5000LY applaud, without any
adoration.
Eye squint, sinister smile, I feel omen.
Promised Land ? ...another episode ?

The prison, the Dancer, why cell her? I ask.
Bartok, piano tutorial small universe, she pregnant.
said Narcissus, save, knee with Kaonashi[1] .

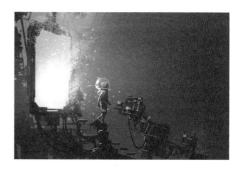

啊！請救贖吧！
Pizza 店老板　道　納西瑟斯
只愛自己的臉
怎知會愛上她？
無臉男　雖如劇　演襯鎝
綿蠺 5000 年　每次換臉

唉！怪我的小試驗　具現化
多重宇宙　異次元的　鎖
又於我有所求？燔祭？又是試品？

交會　老板說　鏡眾求　無鎖　無索　奔流
美好結局　是交會的新宇宙　無所謂的　訴求
再獻祭　你　時間流沙的　纏結　命運的惑魅

允諾之地　你的　她的　我都給 5000 光年的
一串座位

Asked to change another Drama, Pizza Boss spoke.

Narcissus, drown by the love of own face, in love
with her.
Kaonashi, making love as the Bartok drama, but no true
faces.
You, never exist in this mirror, but tangled.
Blame to my test, realization multi lock. Still need
another sacrifice, for all. Pizza Boss spoke.

Will be a new ending, correspond with, the spooky.
Sacrificed your past time sand "Tangled" , let the, Universe,
run, flow, expend, without bound, trapped.

And the promised land, yours, hers, I give them all.

燔祭與結纏

劇《長髮姑娘》（Rapunzel）(1) 是 Pizza 店老板　首選
可再　安定　具現化　宇宙 5000 光年
我燔祭的　是我最愛　時間細砂　界結
贖誰？我的罪？誰的魅？　結局美好的　臉？

Pizza 店老板　收買我　從劇院舞台　看一下座位
第六十七排　中央　十座位　每座位 5000 光年

Anthony Lai

Sonnet | The Miraculous Mandarin 011

Sacrifice concrete and Tangled

My duty to sacrifice the oil paint "Tangle",
as it chooses the same drama tangled from old story
Rapunzel[1].
For salvation, sin ghost, or beauty ended realistic face?
For another 5000LY stable the Universe away from
Bartok. Pizza Boss spoke.

To bribe, see, the 5000 LY[2], ten seats your owned.
In the center of the theater, the lane 67, best position.
Too small ? ahead 20 lanes, 50 thousand LY, 10 seats, hers
and yours.
I trapped, teleportation,
sacrifice my oil paint "Tangled".

To the 2F of the sea food restaurant,
seashore, his waiting with beer and smile.
Better then Sacrifice wait on the Pizza house on Mount
Moriah with Abraham last time.
Made me forgotten, the quantum spooky, space overlapped,
I cut.
The tangle of love, all the past arena.

Good, now the new theater can have a new, correspond.
And the universe does not collapse by the disaster of Bartok.

具現化　宇宙 5000 光年　太小
祂又示好　往前 20 排　每位 5 萬光年　十座位

被惑出賣　又去　海濱　燔祭　我的愛
不用瞬移　出居所　往濱海　如札記　量子　加疊
又是渦漩　就來到了　我燔祭的　漁人碼頭 2F 海產店
加上啤酒　歡笑　勝過
我和亞伯拉罕　摩利亞山 pizza 店　的時節

Pizza 老板　碎鏡面　再具現　去除糾劫
不除　所有宇宙星位　崩裂　也無量子　纏結

我的 創世紀

我　無位　無名　無姓　無性　有臉

祂　帶我出劇院　在濱海　金色沙　消波塊間

燔祭　虛空的時間沙　結　我舉刀

油畫介面　畫布　鏡面具現　二維　量子　宇宙平面

二維？唉！有二維才有三維　祂言

為何不是一維？點？絕對不是　你我　己經　二維

那大霹靂……有誤？

愛因斯坦 (1) 時空有錯？せ……量子…… 是難解的物理

創吧！你的舞台　看你的　酒歌　創世紀

Anthony Lai

Sonnet | The Miraculous Mandarin 012

My genesis

I, no Seat, Name, no Throne, Neuter, but a Face.
It, me, out the theater, seashore, gold sand beach,
between the chopping blocks, sacrifice burn, enumerates oil
canvas.
Mirror me in on the 2 ways dimension universe.

Why two ways? Not a singularity point? Big ban to 3 ways?
Albert Einstein faults[1] ?
You and me Two ways dimension already.
This is quantum spooky, not Physicism.
Create and sing your Brindisi[2] , desired Universe in your
dream.

I... create for most beloved...who...a girl or a woman... ?
Oh, yes, Così fan tutte[3]. Who you love as to show
historically ?

For the sake of your VIP of sacrifice, I offer
Muse[4] , as your whished beauty, she... ?
Knew, the pregnant woman, will never in your universe.
The boss spoke.

She, with the love of Narcissus, with no face man, you never
exist.
Clone the 12 Apostles[5] , from my ribs, for the mission of

我想　造最愛　誰　女人
也對　女人皆如此 (2)……　造誰？　問　歷史？
Pizza 店老闆說　看在你貢獻　燔祭數上 VIP
建議　先造謬思　謬思　女神　最美……
祂　知道……那一個懷孕的女人……不在你宇宙內。

想造　李斯特　巴哈　莫札特　多明哥……隨你
那一個懷孕的女人……屬 Bartok 小宇宙
她最愛　納西瑟斯　或　無臉男　絕不是你

我於是用我的肋骨　克隆　十二使徒 (4)
我沒有克隆　EVA(5) 因為　我仍是
宇宙星海　徬徨的荷蘭人　等待春雷
的　敲門　用妳的　腳步聲

在不可預期的　深夜　期待
可結尾的　Bartok　滿州大人

wait in my Galaxies.

Waiting for the thunder of her Spring steps, knock to the heart of, the Flying Dutchman[6] , seashore, the residence.

To the end of The Miraculous Mandarin of Bartok.

Seashore variegates

濱海札記

俳句|Haiku

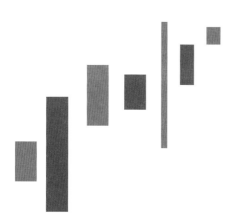

安東尼・賴
俳句 01~03

阿貝渦漩

01

聽窗外淅漓梧桐雨聲

滿杯　阿貝渦漩

醉倒在　無線條的床上　自燃

02

不敢把妳美妙的歌聲比作夜鶯

我的國度沒有夜

只有門框，和地窖尚未熟成的，阿貝渦漩 (1)

03

濱海，巫囚的懷孕女子，臘夜分娩。

產下　多重異次元的　鎖　十四行詩和

地球動脈 混血後　吸入平行時空之黑洞。

Anthony Lai

Haiku 01~03

Abbe Vortex

01

Listen to the sound of Sycamore outside the window.

Cup full of Abbe vortex.

Falling drunk on the bed of empty strip and spontaneously ignite.

02

Dare not compare your beautiful singing to a nightingale.

There is no night in my home.

Only the door frame, and the unmatured cellar-Abbe Vortex.

03

The pregnant woman of a Witcher prisoner, giving birth in Winter night.

Son of multiple locks of different dimensions mixed my Seashore Sonnets.

In the terrestrial arteries, all in the black hole of hybrid time and space.

散文|Prose

房東（信仰與訊息）

landlord

安東尼 · 賴
散文

房東（信仰與訊息）

　　每週一，天微亮，刺耳的吸塵器把夢全吸走。懶散的靈，月光照撫下，揮手道別的勃起都被吸走。可是，有一天早上那刺音成，上帝說：帶著你的最愛，上山燔祭。那天，我遇見，亞伯拉罕，在摩利亞山 (1) Pizza 店。

　　到底，我們是自己的房東？上帝的房客？或者，我們沒有那麼富有，想要允諾，我們是某些人的房客。租房，渡日，曲指餘年？……去阿刻戎河 (2) 擺渡錢，向誰去借？

　　在某夜，晚醉後，醒來，映入她穿著半透的白紗，坐在床沿。啊！初生的早晨，我尚有一點私產，我是她半裸的，荒謬信仰的房東。

　　就牽動回憶到和我弟弟，四十年前，那時他放棄台大某科系，重考，我當兵回來。我們在補課後閒聊，一個叫齊克果 (3) 的丹麥人，有一本書叫《誘惑者日記 (4)》，唉啊！不是誘惑女性，是具現化，荒謬與信仰的逆量子糾結。

　　（齊克果（Søren Kierkegaard）直接地說，亞伯拉罕燔祭獨

Anthony Lai

Prose

landlord

Years on, every Monday morning, piercing sound from vacuum machine, sucked all.

Leased lazy spirits from the moon light waved.

Moreover, erect penis bid farewell.

One day, finally God spoke, burnt offering, up to Moriah[1] .

I met Abraham, that day in the pizza house near the hilltop.

Doubt who are we? landlord of ourselves ? Or roomer of whose God ? Or poor as we rent a room from somebody else. Asking promises ?

Daily paid, even to borrow the Acheron[2] obol.

Mattinata(the morning song), as memorized her half-trans white dresses, between drunk and awake, the only faith I kept is believing someone within me.

Memorized that period of time in years ago, study for re-entrance exam, my brother and I most interesting in discussing the book of "*Forførerens Dagbog*"[3] [4] Of Søren Kierkegaard.

Oh, not how to cheat girls, but faith, believe absurd for abandoning his marriage. The discussion mentioned "absurd beliefs" which realization inverse quantum entanglement.

The only son of Abraham's burnt offering is a belief, and an absurdity. "Everyone can easily understand that it is absurd, but who can understand because of the absurdity and belief ? " Soren spoke.

子乃一信仰，乃一荒謬。「每一個人都能容易了解它是荒謬」，齊克果說：「但因荒謬而信仰有誰能了解呢？」）

幾十年來人生，經歷多重思索，不懂這話，「荒謬而信仰」或信仰荒謬的意思，直到最近我的房客，租了我的心房，我才弄懂。

考慮很久，都不知如何下手寫的哲學思維……只能寫說——從齊克果，跳過黑格爾 (5)、佛洛依德 (6)、拉岡 (7)（跳過夢及潛意識）直接來到，具現信仰的哲學家——斯拉沃熱 · 齊澤克（斯洛維尼亞語：Slavoj Žižek(8)）

他說：他一直很疑惑的一種人，是「企業家」，有很多企業家有錢後，卻投入更多心力到企業，每天競競業業，如神父 每天禱告，與信仰上帝無異，那他們信仰什麼？

當我相信，可以用義大利文唱歌劇詠嘆調，錄成我專輯對身旁的人是種荒謬，到社大找一找，還居然有一位聲樂家，留學義大利七年的女高音，回台教唱。一看課程曲目，居然有兩首在我信仰歌單上。

Mattinata, 及茶花女歌劇中的 brindisi（飲酒歌）。

她本身就是樂器。她的聲音，甜美，有厚度，潔淨無暇的女高音，如晶瑩剔透美鑽，如名琴樂器。

Decade 's life up and down, cannot understand the real meaning, until someone else rent my penthouse.

Thinking over, the only way to express my thoughts is to jump through from Søren, G. W. F. Hegel[5] , Sigmund Freud[6] , Jacques Marie Émile Lacan[7] to the Slavoj Žižek[8] .

He illustrate that the most touch is "one kind of person he has always been puzzled by, is many entrepreneurs who are rich, but they devote more energy to the enterprise, competing in the business every day, like a priest praying every day, which is no different from believing in God."

What do they believe in ?

When I believed in using Italian singing opera arias to record into my album, I realized the difficulty, absurd by others.

Go to the community college to look for it,

There is a vocalist who has studied in Italy for seven years and teaches.

Looking at the course repertoire, there are two on my song list-The Mattinata and Brindisi.

She is a musical instrument.

Her voice is the sweetest, thick, clean high pitch. Such as crystal-clear diamonds, such as famous piano instruments.

Every time it is like listening to the soprano Anna Yuliyevna Netrebko[9] singing in a small indoor palace opera house in Italy.

Free, open, funny, and when I am in a bad mood, evening class makes me joyful.

She taught us to sing opera with our own voice, not to parrot.

Because she believes that such good music must be taught, and someone shall be learned from it.

She is not afraid that students cannot even breathe in, exhale, or make a sound... She accepts everything.

每次，都像在義大利小型室內皇宮歌劇院，聽安娜‧尤利耶芙娜‧涅特列布科 (9) 高歌。

　　自由、開放、風趣，不好心情晚課後就變愉悅。

　　她教我們用自己的聲音唱歌劇，不是去仿出名的歌唱大師。她說，這麼好的音樂，一定要教，一定有人學。

　　不怕收不到學生，不怕學生連吸氣、吐氣、發聲⋯⋯都不會。她全收。

　　教不會唱歌的老人唱歌劇，是具現荒謬。

　　用她的生命，熱情去付出，因為熱愛信仰。

　　無理性、荒謬的，具現催生的「異次元纏結」。

　　我終於從她知道信仰是什麼，荒謬的思想具現或未具現的「荒謬」。

　　聞，被理性謀殺的屍体血腥味「就是摩利亞山 Pizza 出爐的香味」

Teach the 70 years old people singing opera is manifest absurd.

Use her life and enthusiasm to give because she loves everything that in her belief.

Irrational and absurd manifestation spawned a different-dimensional entanglement.

I finally know from them what "faith" is.

That is the mind path on the absurd or the absurd working on the rotten body of faith. No matter what, path is everything.

It is Mount Moriah Pizza fragrance.

濱海札記

十四行詩|sonnet

安東尼 · 賴
十四行詩 007

房　客

唉！　請接受這份讚禮　不是交易
風塵僕僕　僕僕風塵　被吹來這裡
想停車也得找車位　也得拉手煞
暫置心蹼引擎　也得打 par

貧乏　倦怠　乏人問津的歲月
像模像樣商品　卻賣不出去
唉啊！　妳得相信　是「信仰」的行為
也是誓言

浮士德　如是梅菲斯托菲勒斯　的借客
那我　就是上帝的⋯⋯房東
只不過　想向「瑪格麗特」祈求碇泊
每次禱告　都簽下「告白」的醉約

賃妳心房閣樓　給我吧！我按日交租抵押　餘年
「Diabolus」附的身　「Blasphemy」借的魂　而這贈禮　是
「Muse」給的桑田

Anthony Lai

Sonnet 007

roomer

Alas! please accept this gift, no trade, innermost being.
Pneumatic mind with dusty body, be here.
Try to find a parking lot, like sediment within the blood
syringe.
Hand brake my beating heart engine.

Deficient life, weary sensation, lake of foison from touch.
I, as a good-looking merchandise, found no price sold.
My dear, this is concern about the Faith.
Moreover to say, a promising.

濱海札記

Faust[1] contract sold heaven to Mephistopheles[2] for 24 years.
Then I shall be the landlord of my providence.
I pray for anchorage in the harbor of Marguerite, everytime with futile drunk.
Just rent the penthouse to me, daily pay, mortgage rest life mine.

Diabolus possessed, Blasphemy soul, but this gift, sacrament of Muse.

散文|Prose

給一個懷孕的女人
To a pregnant woman

安東尼 · 賴
散文

給一個懷孕的女人

2020 年九月， 在淡水濱置駐居所，無意中遇到一個懷孕的女人，有某種非常迷人的美，感覺她似乎從某個幸福的「宇宙蟲洞」中，誕生出來。

我非常著迷於她的雙眼，真實的看著你，在對話的時侯，率真不作忸態。

她懷孕卻又無初孕的興奮，工作辛苦，但卻總微笑以對。她說她已經是二個孩子的母親，一男一女。年長的都二十歲了，爾後閑聊中又得知，現在腹中懷的是改嫁後再孕……

Anthony Lai

Prose

To a pregnant woman

Someday in the September of 2020, settled an apartment to the seashore. Coincidently met the pregnant woman with charming beauty. The beauty seems come from her happiness living which created from unknown worm hole, another Universe against mine.

I am so fascinated with her eyes, look at you directly through your soul, conversation with the words from her mind directly enable get your true response.

You can feel that her exciting with something which is not pregnancy of the baby, but expecting another living concerned with the new birth will be.

Harding working, always smiling, here now is the happiness itself.

She said she had two children already, a 20 year old daughter and a 19 years old son.

I asked why pregnant in your age of 40.

Yes, she said when he grown up, I am 60 years old.

The question seems no need to answer to, afterward I knew, the pregnancy from her new marriage.

It is just a common salary job, I barely seen no social engraved, no living wrinkles, no job pressures invaded at her face but enjoying.

Future concern, confused with life, wondering path of sinister of new marriage....

Fearless spread out the instantaneous doubt, seems Nona (Clotho) [1] already spinning her yarn of fate, why fear Thanatos.

她的工作收入不多，臉上卻完全沒有被工作、歲月，消蝕的刻痕。未來，她說：是的，等「他」二十歲成年，我都已經六十歲了。

　　擔憂困惑只在她 眼中閃過，似命運之神 (1) 已經眷戀過，Thanatos 死神，有何懼？

　　動作優雅的清潔碗盤，恰如曾經，美滿生活的縮影，物質上，不可能培育率真；一定是生活中心靈的盈滿，才能養生出的優雅。

　　感覺得到，在工作中準備食材，清洗、烹調、收拾，對她而言不像工作，是過去正在訴說的寫真。

　　幾首十四行詩的靈感來自，她問：為什麼來淡水海濱駐居，她說，我家世居淡水，生在淡水，嫁給淡水人，卻不覺淡水迷人，我提到曾旅遊過的歐州……拿波里……

　　在希臘……迷人的海濱，島嶼，居所，陽光，如畫美景沙灘……。

　　她只是笑一笑，似乎正對我說：呆子，那只是人和心情的感情懷影，駐居，就不見得如是了。

　　我在逃離過去塌陷的時空，追尋。謬思未來，我還在 尋覓居所？或是，我為了尋找更自由的居所，想讓未來，更用力推開過去？如同「暗物質」正用力在分離星系。

　　徬徨的荷蘭人 Van der Decken(2)

Cooking, cleaning dishes, the graceful attitude from nature reactions of living. Seems dip into pasture life of kitchen.

It is not emerged from materiality but psychic of past.Preparing meals, cleaning table, is a portraiture.

It is very strange that some Sonnet poetry of Seashore variegates from her questions, why come to here and buy the residence ?

Living in Tamsui, bone here, married local man, never felt any charming here. She spoke. I replied that been in Europe, Napoli, Greek…the seashore…the beaches…the island, not there but here, I believe can reflect something analogy.

She was smiling, seems said: you are slow witted, it is vague for emotions. Living is another matters.

I am trying to run away my limited past, nor to say, exhausted good past but suffocated.

Searching for the future residence to free from current frame, or new residence can push harder.

As the darkness matters makes each Galaxy away and spacing my Universe. She revoked me thinking of the Opera of

The Flying Dutchman, if I become Van Der Decken(2) ?
Then who is she ?

如果是我？那她又會是誰？

十四行詩|sonnet

Seashore variegates

安東尼・賴
十四行詩　001

居　　所

妳曾問我　　從何處來　　將何處去
為何愛海　　雨驟鷗跡渺　　浪淘沙無痕
半生稜陌　　己成滄海　　墨旱篇離
光陰蝕鏽　　春霖喚不回　　秋瀬織夢醇

迴盪著　　疑慮的聲音　　牽絆微鎖的眉頭
何曾相識　　彩霓的雙眸　　獨有的唯美
乍然間　　遙遠的泊魂　　靄靄塵封裡的我
遍尋不著　　虛空的理由　　嘆息的纏結

徬徨荷蘭人向我招手　　卻仍停泊並惆躕步履
她的心已然新孕填滿　　我將面臨寒冬的冷冽
就在海濱找個駐居所　　保存破碎的些許回憶
在流散中看時間的海　　等著敲打門扉的春雷

Anthony Lai

Sonnet 001

Residence

You asked where came from and shall go ?
Why love sea, seagulls gone for rain drops as foot marks for
the tide.
Life among ridge, either raise or tide drop, luscious tone
flutter and fall.
Spring tears hard recall, only Autumn shore dream orbit by.

輟遲裝修的緣由　是怕伴海風吹來的希望
皆已腐朽
可是卻又在妳微笑中　我見到的　是海天
盛宴的宇宙

Wishful eyebrow, question with eager sound, echo in concourse.
Your sole beauty with spirit eyes, seems my memories knew.
My stray soul, stub lifestyle, suddenly, no longer of because.
As the empty breast, reasons of sigh, become a well tune.

Van der Decken waved, still lounge and wondering stumble feet.
Her heart felt with expecting, mine be frozen by the coming Winters' cold.
Live, looking into the waves, wait the knock door sound may abrupt.
For the broken string of bygone, could be rewind.

Decorated yet, fear hopes could decay from the wind of sea, but in your smile, there are blues and stars crave thee.

74

濱海札記

十四行詩|sonnet

002　巫囚

002 Medea

(I met a clone prisoned

by a crone)

安東尼・賴
十四行詩 002

巫　囚

從　頹廢弦維　被瞬移到　一座城堡　似乎在　居所　濱海的盡頭
囚著　蒙眼　懷孕的女人　我問緣由　美狄亞 (1) 說　她懷了　宇宙
掀開外衣　她橢圓　外凸的　透明　肚皮內　納著　數不清的　星斗
何時　竊得了　愛的蟲洞　具現　有性生殖的
結索

巫說　在某星系　不是窗裡外的　第幾重　而是悸動
她吸入了世上　煩擾疑惑　再用光束　吐回　成　匯流
不知將　何去何求　生出　多重異次元的　鎖　或　秋雨梧桐
我蹲下　撫一下肚皮　整個人　被吸入　又回　到　居所

總是沙漏　翻轉無由　再遇見那蒙眼的女人　從我的鏡界　克隆
是虛我　的　繾綣　是實我　的　欲語還休　或　幻愛的　疑惑
現存世紀有誰？　在乎故事　坑洞　別瞎說　能不能愛的　因果
那思念　結成氤塵　在弦維訴說　纏結　是異次元的　妳我

Anthony Lai

Sonnet 002

Medea
(I met a clone prisoned by a crone)

From the lifetime string moved to a castle, seems at the shore
end of my living residence.
Prisoned, a pregnant a woman pregnant my corer.
I asked the crone, said, she have a baby of the Universe.
A thousand of star galaxy in her belly, when I open her cloth
shelter.
She Stored the love worm hole, by when? came to the new
blank DNA verse.

而那巫女　愉悅的　囚著未懷孕的　克隆　說　我不知愛憐
只會刑咎
我問　因何又變回　巫囚　美狄亞卻說　你不知　她已經
懷著「消瘦」

Crone said, in galaxies, not in/out her window curtains, but
heart quaker.
She absorbed all doubts and wonders, binds throwback to
starlight stream.
The birth be a multiple universe lock or a Sycamore flower.
I hugged the surface, and all in sucked, back onto the
residence redeem.

Always seashore time sand, turned, see the blind clone taken
out of my mirror.
Once lived in my cocoons, beyond love, or hesitate
expression.
The fruit of thinking, the twingle of fate, yours and mine
interfered.
Who, care about the tale? Not say, time results to love
amortization.

And the Medea prison the clone again, and said.
I prison them all, why ? Don 't you know that she already
pregnant
"thin therefore" ?

濱海札記

十四行詩|sonnet

003-r1 螺蹤物語
003-r1 obscured love

安東尼・賴
十四行詩 003-r1

螺蹤物語

某夜　步出居所　在海濱漫步　不見砂漏　只聆　浪戛
幔幃　夜幕中　遇見　那懷孕的女人　與我　擦身而過
她停下卻步回首　與我　再次邂逅　那夜　大雨漫沱
靜寂地支之七　卻見　滿天星愁　我銀河的
漩渦

某日某月　步出砂漏　卻不見濱波
只秧得深秋
礁岩中　遇見　那拾螺的女人
意願　共尋螺蹤
目光焦灼　卻沒停下　拾得　瓶中信　已在
十萬光年後
夢結線手　惑在　量與逆量　皆具現　在　無垠的　潮間帶中

某年　某月　某日　不見螺貝
只見　無色　碎玻
沙灘裡　遇見　那個畫沙的女人　正向

Anthony Lai

Sonnet 003-r1

obscured love

That night, clepsydra gone, walking by my seashore, only
waves pounce.
Mantle of darkness, the pregnant woman passed by.
Abrupt stop her path, evoke, and doubt encounter? rain,
inundated tearful nights ?
Noon! the seventh earthly branches, my solitary galaxy
vortex, not your tide.

Days and months stepped out sand glass, nothing but
mosaic autumn.
Among ridges, met a snail picker, ask for
collaborate with.
Hesitated, until found the bottle letter, already thousands
of years anthem.
Fantasy in between spooky real and unreal, in the dreamed
tidal zones.

Months and years, Cassandra[1] prophecy, met her on the
shore sole.
I did not see the conch, but broken glasses without color.
A woman narrates, sand painting, always in mind the past
episode.
It is dark matters perturbed, we never kissed on that time
polar.

卡珊德拉 (1) 訴說

沙繪　過往的　緣由　它　不放手

皆是　暗物質　攪動　我們在

光陰迴波中　不曾吻過

都怪　諸神說　可是　哲理說

願為　倫常事理　箇囚

又何必　在海濱　漫步中

無緣無由

欲語　還休

Blame to the God said, people said, and or sage said, as prisons of ethics.
No reasons why looking onto the eyes each other with obscured lovense.

十四行詩|sonnet

安東尼 · 賴

十四行詩　004

現代生活

有一個祈求的聲音，出現在一首歌裡，那歌可成
詩篇
有二韻淒涼，出現同在一段文字裡，那文字就變
訴求
有三片落葉，飄落在淺池塘裡，那池塘就代表
漣漪
而有四支電扇，同時置在房裡，懶散風吹絕對是
龍捲

有一種似是而非在電視裡，那積非就烙　成了
真理
有二隻青蛙在那塊稻田裡，呼然子夜就　有了
鄰居
有三個商店開在同條街裡，那某條街就　成了
市集
而同時有四個溜狗人在公園裡，「踏到」就

Anthony Lai

Sonnet 004

modern life

A forbid sound, found in the ballad, rhyme turn into a
poem.
Two chilly words in a paragraph, the paragraph become a
beseech.
Three leaves fall into the pond, where ripples begin to stim.
Four fans piping in the same room, the lazy wind turn into
stormish.

A non-true broadcasting on TV, soon the false chrome to
sincerite.
Two frogs in the same territory, nights oblige loud neighbor.
Three stores opened at the same street, the street into clawed
market.
Four dogs' feces at the green park same time, tread shall be
probable.

A man and woman in love, forever become no determine.
Two beds who belongs, plunder is the fruit of linden.
Three buses into the same stand, careful, which you step in.
Four friends drinking at same table, sensory become the key
to vibrating.

A pregnant woman told me: No Line platform? How you
survive in lives ?
Well, canorous alone, may be good for my health.

天經地獄

曾有一些時侯愛上某人，那些時侯注定是
天長地久
就算有二個不同的床頭，那掠奪便是
菩提樹結的果
某時段　有三輛公車同時到站，那上哪就得
瞬息定蹴
而某夜四個朋友同桌喝酒，酒品便成了
決裂的緣由

有個懷孕的女人告訴我，沒有 line
你怎麼活？
那在這座都市鬣林裡，圖清靜怎麼不是種
重要享受

俳句|Haiku

安東尼・賴
俳句 01~03

雪 與 耶誕節

01

螢幕預言 大屯山 可能冬夜雪

火堆烤著 在倦唱 波西米 小手冷血 [1]

天明後 陽光耀眼 逐放 曖昧

02

為什麼？耶誕節 這裡 從不下雪

走不動的 馴鹿雪橇 年年堆疊

床頭依舊懸著 老紅襪 裝著 皺紋詩頁

03

在沒了聖誕樹屋塔內 廣播 聖誕樂

會不會 U-BER 禮物？怕我還在冬眠

不會 只給 有夢童孩 你夢的 蠶編織著

Anthony Lai

Haiku Poetry 01~03

Christmas and Snow

01

TV broadcasting, Datun$_{(1)}$ hill be first Winter snow.
Nightgale aside with rocked fire,
singing La Boehme $_{(2)}$, bloody cold touch.
Daybreak, the sun is dazzling and exile ambiguous.

02

Why it never snows here in the Christmas night ?
Immobile reindeer sleigh piles up by years.
The pillar still hangs the old red socks with wrinkled poem pages.

03

Broadcast Christmas music in the Tower House without bubbly tree,
Will it be a U-BER gift? Afraid, I am still hibernating.
No. only for the dream child, silkworm still not finish yours yet.

濱海札記

十四行詩|sonnet

安東尼 · 賴

十四行詩　005

曲　　線

曲線──女子低頭看手機的　　　曲線多美
晚禮服蕾絲半露雙峰的　　　　曲線多美
流星掠過夜空天際　短暫光弧　曲線多美
比不上那懷孕女人肚子凸起的　曲線美

臉的輪廓有很多美麗的曲線　沒有愛慾交會的　　　曲線美
妙齡女子緊身衣褲　曲線美不美？沒有插秧農婦的　曲線美
心為歡愛　上下起伏的　悸動心電圖　測得到的期待　曲線美
短裙　防窺視　交叉的曲線　沒有分娩　雙腿分開時的　曲線美

常在想　羅浮宮內　在蒙那麗莎旁　掛幅　瑪丹娜
年輕裸照　誰比較美？
青春不用繪　無可比的美
但接吻時　那雙唇線　再也不美
舌纏的曲線最美

被月光脫下的衣服　捲曲……危美
做愛完後　蘿夢是美　缺憾是美　再回到現實生活　美不美？

Anthony Lai

Sonnet 005

curve

A girl down her head reading network, beautiful curve.
Woman ware V neck dresses, beauty breast curved.
Meteor across the night sky, short light beauty curve.
More beauty be the pregnant woman belly curved.

At the moment of love and sex, climax face curves.
Teenaged with shapeware, how beauty the body curved.
Dating the love, heart beating diagram, course of events.
Short skirt, across legs, the curves cannot compare birthing legs
open curved.

Thinking of hang, a necked youth Madonna by Monalisa,
in Musée du Louvre. Which more attractive ?
It is no need picture to draw the youth, all in side walkway.
When kiss, the lips line pressed, not beauty, the tangled tone is
tumbtive.

Moon night serenade took her cloth off, curved body in reality.
Ravished, dream is stil hanging, do not ask, awaked sensility.

濱海札記

十四行詩|sonnet

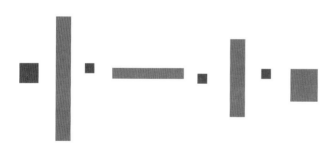

安東尼 · 賴
十四行詩　006

我於是上了捷運

那，喧嘩，不是，是低讀，吟唱，四方機的祈福門檻。
回，些什麼？音訊？情人只有眼神，唉！文字——多痴。
尋，新聞？車禍，家暴，倫背，偷情……啊……閒聊最愛。
看，字眼就，興奮，妄猜，飯後私約，定上了——魔鐵。

中古世紀鐵匠磨的鐵，很硬，但也很脆，加太多心血。
那捷運還有什麼？嫩白的腿，糟透，說是偷拍行為？
東櫻裙短，唐規現隋，但滿城罂煙何處在？
哦！大飯店——豪帖。
處一室，求鴛鴦契約，城市蠢林匪類，蚰之又是誰？

我自家門前千堆血，卻非管他，虛無的瓦上關，　無解。
我腳鐐，雙手銬踭又如何？輕飄上了——人權——「大安站」
我換了幾線捷運，又回到黃線「永安市場站」誰奈何？
自由女神像（Statue of Liberty）蒙不蒙眼，掉淚？

Anthony Lai

Sonnet 006

thus I turn onto the sub

That is clamors, no, it is slogan mumble rat for digital phone.
Braille responds for love ? Eye, non expression.
News, crash car, home, marriage..., gossips to chart with.
Exciting about the thinking of Motel, after lunch meal.

Motel stroke weapons for sex battles, too much in blood.
More on the sub, shoot tender legs, sinister way.
Tokyo short skirt harassment, old dynasty toxic.
Toxic relations, in 5 star's hotel room, girls wait upon.

Bloody snow, we care only neighbor's housetop.
Human right for crimes, I will be on safe subway station.
And I turn to another line to no offence stops
Who care about the Libertas blind eye tears ?

Liberty fire never burn under the judiciary frame.
Law books casing the ignitions, middle finger speaks.

光睢倒影的閃動為誰？她那手持的火炬從未燒燃，

是什麼？法律畫冊的亮光，誰是誰非的──「比中指」的灼爛

安東尼・賴
十四行詩 015

愛 之 夢

將妳身體　姿擬　名琴 piano Bosendorfer
而我　妳的虛無情人　李斯特
哦！不是　月光掠過　微風輕撫　彈著
仿！他的靈魂　用力敲打　時空　崩塌

不願 把妳美妙的歌聲　比作　夜鶯
我在的國度　沒有　夜　牠尋不著
陽光下　無歌　累歇著　那就用喉　咕嚕的
停我掌上　啄食歲月　把手心染成金黃

妳的國度　我　如飲　燒酎　如　鳩渴　如　信鴿　自由翱翔
我的國度　不要造訪　雙足在煉金師爐內　己成岩炭
拿下我心臟內的　賢者之石　身體為　消波塊
在濱海札記中　衝擊　撿拾泡沫足跡

我仍舊歡喜
我等著那一隻海鷗　可能的駐立

Anthony Lai

Sonnet 015

Liebesträume(1)

Make a metaphor to your body, a piano Bosendorfer[2] ,
and I, pretend your nonentity lover Liszt.
Moonlight and breeze flicks, not my manner.
Imitates his soul, beating hard, time and space collapse.

I don't want to compare your singing to a nightin.
The zone I am in, has no night, birds taciturn.
Scorch by the sun, tired and rest, only throat Grumbling.
Stop on my palm, pecking at my past, dye the palms of my hands
in
golden.

As drinking Shochu[1] , as toxic dreams, as a pigeon soaring freely
under your arms.
Not visit my residence, both feet had become rock coal in the
alchemist furnace.
Take the sage stone out of my heart, body turnes into blocks.
Shock and pick-up foam footprints in my seashore variegates.

I am still delighted.
I am waiting for that seagull to stand.

濱海札記

十四行詩｜sonnet

016 平行時空
016 parallel cube

安東尼・賴
十四行詩 016

平行時空

妳在午後兩點十三分　三點三三三……　秒　躺著
看著凸圓的肚子又往下掉了大約　零點三三三公分
我在午後小睡打烊著　但那鼾聲卻咕嚕嘛著
看著夢中凸起的詩泡陽具　大約也只長了零點幾公分

走到　烏金髮　稻禾　飄散的　田裡
有隻　懷孕的麻雀　躺在我手掌裡
禾手裡當作巢　產下兩顆　草鴞　紋蛋
有顆似　仙女星系的　紋盤
另一顆是　銀河的　棒嵐　三十億光年後的
碰撞　是分合　離散　或　終始的結纏

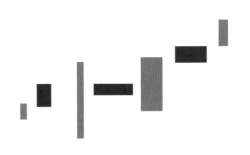

Anthony Lai

Sonnet 016

parallel cube

You lie expectation down at 2:13 in the afternoon, 3.3333…
second.
Looking at your delivery cargo drop about 0.333cm.
And I took a nap in the afternoon , emotion closed, but the
snoring sound murmured.
Looking at the protruding poem phallic in my dream, it
only grew by a few tenths of a centimeter…

平行時空　平行宙宇　也是平行著的　海濤和麻辣鍋　鴨血
我凸起的思緒　妳肚皮內隆起的漪漣　是不平行的　物語
我跨不出棒漩銀河的主星系　妳也拋不掉仙女座的　螺居
光年　是淡水冬雨唱著娩觴　產房掛著的　滴點

我在午後兩點十三分　三點三三三四秒醒來
卻發現　醉在老枯藤纏的　紅酒窖中
喝著初桶的　薄酒萊

When I walked into your black hair, rice grains, enchanted scattered fields,
there was a pregnant sparrow lying in the palm of my hand.
As a nest and laid two grass owl eggs.
Andromeda Galaxy center spiral, and the other is the Milky Way's bar.
The collision three billion light years later are a separation, reunion, or entanglement at the end.

Parallel to time and space, to Universe, also parallel, sea wave of spicy pot, and duck blood.
I cannot cross the frame of the galaxy, and you can't throw away the spiral Andromeda dwelling.
My raised thoughts, the ripples in your belly,
are unparalleled.
It's Tamsui Winter rain singing the birthing goblin,
hanging in the delivery room, light years dropping.

I woke up at 2:13 in the afternoon, 3:3334 seconds.
But I found that drunk in the wine cellar of old grape vine tangled Beaujolais [1].

Seashore variegates

詩|Poetry

孕母
Matrix

安東尼・賴
詩

孕　母

總在回想之後
分割時空　切細　那回憶才就更　具體
就是瞬間
妳手指　指著　該簽的　蛹藏　位置

裴意　用食指　觸碰
連著　沒有力氣　移開
看著　妳眼　在說　簽吧　似是我的　租約
DNA 透過手指的　無限聯結

順著手指　一直向上望　延伸到　妳的臉
是絕對　完美的　曲線　我的笑　妳的　燦爛　炸開了　空氣中
疏生的　煤岩炭煙的　油脂味
熔了　虛空中　秦朝兵俑　僵屍棺材　的　疊堆

我的　平行宙宇　生了
銑陽星糸　恆星──她　星軌──我。

Anthony Lai

Poetry

Matrix

Cast my mind back to the core of memories.
Revolve, and cut that time into tiny streams.
It is becoming realization of the seconds.
Here, both fingers touch the allusion point, forever's being.

Irresolute, hard to move away, but look at your eyes, seems
speak that sign here.
It is your contract rental, your spooky DNA tangled with
mine.
My stingless network online from now on.

Looking upon from finger to your face,
a perfect curve extends.
The smiles of yours and mine blooming which burst out
rusty, and melt zombie overlapped heart.

A small bright galaxy formed in my universe.
Her solar and my spacecraft obit.
The crone speaks, she will bone multi universe of yours in
this residence.

I finally able to go back to the residence of childhood.
Clearly seen father's young smiles on his new motobike.

巫囚說　她懷著　宇宙　會生出　異次元　的　多重　居所。

我終於　可以回到　童年的住所
就此　我清楚看見　父親臉上清淅的　微笑線條
滿足的　騎在　六十五年前　最愛的　機車上
母親　年青貌美　浮現

父親和我弟　下棋悠閒
我的　歌劇　黑膠唱片　阿飄的媚眼　阿杜的　裸體速寫 (1)

咖啡　小菜　濁酒　四十年前
新樂園的　香煙味
啊！散漫　台南　鐵路旁　蝸居　我最深邃的　憶

那囚巫　啃掉　我時光的殼　喝了陳年的　威士忌　噫語：生下
在地球 DNA 的子
他的濱海──十四行詩，子夜的玫瑰　預言的
銀河史詩──新　伊里亞德　奧德塞
成為　孕母

The evocation of my mother's beauty face and father playing chess with my brother long ago.

My opera disk records, float charming eyes, the sketch of resistless woman body.
Coffee, appetizer, turbid sake, the smoking smells in 1970's.
Oh! unruly time period used in my life, in Tainan, the residence of my sister's, but memories mine.

That crone, ate my shell of life, drunk by my whiskeys, and speaks.
Her DNA son and your Sonnet seashore variegates and the Nocturnal rose.
Prophetic novel, new galaxy, Iliad, and Odyssey.
And she became Matrix.

Seashore variegates

濱海札記

俳句|Haiku

01~05 廊前燕

01~05 swallow

安東尼・賴
俳句 01~05

廊前燕

01

草鴞問冰雪　結凍時間　成名後　感覺

黑面琵鷺　道盡北域凜冽　濕地下午茶會

雪白玉肌　碧眼朱唇　媚外　保育類

02

廊前燕　不再回　擊鼓告春天

雨延綿　佇立望眼　紅綃咽綠

應蟬　蛙啼　月夜醉　坼簷緣

03

簷內多泥巢　廊前無燕歸　誰舉杯？

南國冬暖　鶯聲美　燕不歸

夜未眠　空巢　無詩　澤遷

04

昨夜　風疏雨驟　落枝凝殘酒

Anthony Lai

Haiku Poetry 01~05

swallow

01

Grass owl asks the freezing time of north land ice.
Famous, Black-faced Spoonbill$_{(2)}$, bitter tails, worm afternoon tea tweetup.
As foreign advantage priority protection.

02

Galleries swallow no longer returns, drumming to suit Springs.
Red silk cry to the greens, rain arrest swallow back.
Only can echo cicada, frog cry, moon night drunk, tear eaves.

03

So many mud nests in the eaves, and no swallows back porch.
Who toasts with ?
Warbler in warm south, why north?
Sleepless at night, empty nest, no poetry, re-dwelling.

04

Last night, sparse wind with hard rained, twigs drunk.
Title to the nest, swallow fall on my palm.
Sleep together, making love with Spring years.

唧為巢　廊前燕醉　掉在我掌上
用手捧著　同眠 春天的歲月

05
是詩詞說的　廊前燕歸　暖夜？
春邀約　誰家塵封燕　被贖回？
高原騎士 (2)　在高原　揮手
雪莉桶內的　十八年

05

Who's poem saying swallows returns, at the warm night ?
Spring invitation, whose dusty swallow was redeemed.
Highland Park$_{(2)}$ wave, drunk in sherry bottle 18 years.

126

濱海札記

散文|Prose

煮飯花
Mirabilis

安東尼 · 賴
散文

煮飯花

　　孩提時眼裡的煮飯花，在嘉義鄉間佈開，是媽媽囑託的訊息，在外面玩到傍晚時，看野外小徑上的煮飯花開了，是媽媽在煮飯了。

　　要快步回家哦！媽媽花時間把我們洗淨，才能上餐桌，是爸爸唯一的要求。

　　我不太在意飯菜香，卻常在意，想著，為何在那時花會開。

　　也有煮飯花開，媽媽沒有煮飯，爸爸高興著，到新營市場餐廳吃日本料理，也有時吵架，媽媽哭回娘家，就……記憶中，少有煮飯花開，吃不到飯。

　　母親是把愛透過在嘴上吟著，記不得她是否有抱著我 疼過，就像我再怎麼愛也無法抱著痛哭，只流淚握她的手，看她離去。

　　姊姊說，爸爸發脾氣時，吃飯會掀桌子，我少有印象，只記得，他都在樓下診療替人看病。或許他發脾氣時，母親把小孩推進其他房關了起來，以免波及。

　　爸爸走後，母親在弟弟照看下又獨自生活二十年，不習慣北部，天氣及車馬喧囂，即使有替她備新房，她寧活在舊房

Anthony Lai

Prose

Mirabilis

The cooking flower always looks the same in the eyes of childhood was blooming in the countryside of Chiayi. It's a message from my mother played outside until the evening, when I watched the cooking flowers bloom on the wild trails.

It is my mother who is cooking.

Go home quickly.

Mother took time to wash us before on the dinner table, It is the only request from Dad. I don't really care about the smell of food.

But I always care, thinking, why the flowers will bloom at that time.

Sometimes, cooking flowers blooming, mother did not cook, Dad was so happy that went to the Xinying restaurant near the market, to eat Japanese cuisine.

Sometimes quarrels, my mother cries back to her natal home, just... In my memory, there are very few cooking flowers blooming, and dinner table was empty.

Mother was puffing love through her mouth, could not remember her love hugs.

It's like I can't hold and cry no matter how much I love, I just take her hands in tears and watch her leave.

My sister said that when Dad loses his temper, he probably raise the dinner table. I have little impression, I just remember, he was all downstairs for his patient.

Maybe my mother pushes the children to another

rooms closed, avoided affective.

間屋頂下不離去。

　　近來我年歲愈大，卻常想我那時，是不是忽略了煮飯花開的時間及香味。在她年輕理家煮飯時，會不會是心靈的求救訊號。

　　幾年前，與一串人同遊武漢，在施工路邊，看到湮漫塵埃中，幾株白色煮飯花盛開著，太太在我耳邊低聲叫道，啊喲，看那些是母親口中的煮飯花，也在這時開，不知當地叫什麼花？

　　旅遊回來後，找到一些種子，在陽台上種了幾盆。

　　現在我孫子都記得，叫這種花「煮飯花」。

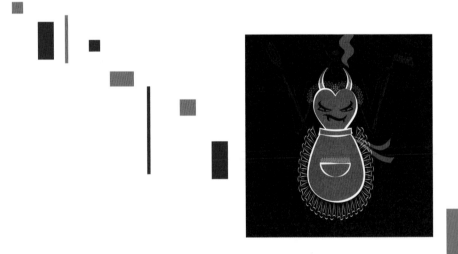

After my father left, my mother lived alone for another 20 years under the care of my younger brother.

Not used to the north I live, the weather and the hustle, she would rather live under the roof of the old room.

Recently, I am getting older and older, but I often think about why the blooming me at that time, did i gnore the time and fragrance of the cooking time flowers ?

Could it be her soul's distress signal ?

A few years ago, traveling with a bunch of people, on the side of the construction road, in the dust, several white Mirabilis are in full bloom My wife whispered in my ear, oh yo, Cooking flowers ! mother mentioned, also blooming at this time, Don't know what flower is called locally ?

After returning from the trip, I found some seeds and planted a few pots on the balcony.

Now my grandsons remembers, this Mirabilia called cooking rice flower, it was called also by your great grandmother.

132

濱海札記

雙十四行詩│Twin Sonnet

1-0&1-1 我曾擁有的美麗相思樹
1-0&1-1 my Acacia tree once before

安東尼 · 賴
雙十四行詩　1-0&1-1

我曾擁有的美麗相思樹
十四行詩 1-0

曾經在我私擁田林裡，有棵茂密的相思樹；
在持有這片，靜謐前，它蕩漾枝葉　就已然舒展　完美。
是誰？把長年培栽之美樹，連地售給我？
大自然彩繪，替它條葉上妝，當夏天來臨時。

暗綠老葉，配上梢頭青翠、新綠，點綴淡黃小花，繽紛溢盈；
小花迎接微風撫過，顫抖著慢慢，飄落在綠茵，草野；
溫柔地，蓋在草地上，她的手，輕撫我，孩提－殤之遺憶。
在樹灣，蔭裡，漫流著，被喚醒的，無憂──是多年傷挫的療藥。

它自然高傲成長著，養分來自於，大地的雨滴及朝露；
我並不需要用太多時間照料，澆灌呵護；
我美麗的相思樹，深根盤纏在深土中；
吸吮地塹之汲滲，和仍依留地底的椿庭、棺槨的筑息。

那個夏天，炙燒數月無雨的曰子裡，我也不認為它會枯萎，
粗率的冷漠，自我放縱；天真的以為，它從不饑竭、不被熾灼。

Anthony Lai

Twin Sonnet 1-0&1-1

my Acacia tree once before
Sonnet 1-0

once a prosper Acacia tree, lives in my private field,
before I owe this tranquil, branches beautifully outstretched.
who ? cultivates this beauty so well, and sold me land ?
all the tress covered up with nature colors in Summer.

elder dark greens, new tops and amber flowers suffused,
the yellow buds fall, bind trembled under smooth wind,
gentle paved the weeds as her hand touching my childhood,
harbored under the shady, for years, cure as medicated.

grown loftily fertilized by rain drops and morning syrup,
needless cherished even not need to irrigated,
my Acacia roots inveterate underground so deep,
sucking rips and coffin of my fathers' dissolve fluid .

that months burnt Summer with my unconcerned,
rough indifference, self-indulgence; naively thinking that it
never gets hungry or burn.

十四行詩 1-1

是從冷氣吹出的嬌涼，啤酒泡沁之狂歡，歡唱著的弦歌
耆友的訪，無間的忙，閒散的謊，擇商之利，而棄的諾；
衍纏的棄捨；竊喜著的無知－相信它通常自然存活。
不知等著，忍著，盼著，是平安的訊，如絲泉之旱霖。

某日酒後　晨醒，悸慄心中的是「八十九元　基本水費」
驅車直上田林，撥開漫草，呆滯凝望這　地獄景況，
乾凋萎槁的　相思樹，葉落枝離　折墜；地面溝裂
盤根大半已經離土，而樹已半傾，如患重瘁。

我拚命澆水，如切開自己的動脈，染紅再生；把樹用椿頂立，
沒查覺－殘留地裡的樹根，已鬆離大地的牽絆。
徹夜設置水管，掘土分向插埋，讓自己相信明天嫩芽再生。
妄想在一夜間，滋潤乾渴的千年。

那一天午夜在加護病房床前，看到滿是紋溝的臉；銀灰荒白
的散髮，對應藍枕，正如我枯槁的樹，淚映著藍空。

cool air, chant songs with beer blister in house,
old friends visit, busy, lazy, too hot, for business sake…
ignorant delight makes me believe naturally survives,
unknown 'visiting' is the only stream she waited.

aroused by the 89 dollars water fee in a morning,
drove to my fiel, hack weed, I saw the hell,
ground crack, uprooted without leaves, half slant.

arterial watering hopes re-bone can be occurred,
straight salvage vain for roots departed already,
bury and conduct pipes new morn green, believed,
fantasize in one night eniough for nourish thirst millenary.

that mid-night looks your grooved face in front of ICU bed,
blue pillow dispersed silver hair as dying Acacia against sky,
jesting ducts in mouth, nose, vein, injects my blood and my
expiateless remorse.

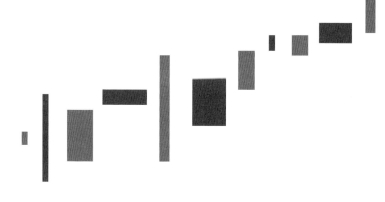

而從鼻，從口，從靜脈管中，不斷的灌澆思念的血泉，嘲諷著──永無法喚回的──歉悔。

十四行詩|sonnet

1-2 子夜的玫瑰

1-2 Rosey Nocturne

安東尼 · 賴
十四行詩 1-2

子夜的玫瑰

子夜彌撒的玫瑰　早就枯萎　留下無法呼吸的音迴
將朽崩的牆　無框窗內　陽光隙照下　盛開刺荊紅華
無言的溫擺　風在訴說　似孤殤的怨對
石桓卻說　是被遺忘的淚水一　蝕刻著我們的　思戀

曾幾何時　孤獨變成　無可選擇的　最愛
把歲月寫在　四方屋內　把光陰烙在　光年之外
究竟　寂寞樹　枝繁葉茂　由於妳對我們　的　思念
或是　我們　無視的　回應　築成的　荒蕪？

我的母親啊！我多麼愚蠢　竟希覬的　期待　妳的淚
可驅趕走我成硬木的　心霉　當我無端默然離去
不熟悉的擁抱　是久別南北的　疏憶　或是　居心叛疑？
期待　絕對未曾符合的　對比　總是　口是心非的　蠱迷
乾枯河川不再期待　春霖　那誰又是誰的　索　拉住奔流

最後摸著　無心跳　的手　是惜我泯淚的最後　訴求　啊！
……散落的咎。

Anthony Lai

Sonnet 1-2

Rosey Nocturne

Rosey withered long ago, leaving a nocturne that cannot breathe.
Decayed wall, frameless window, brush by the sunlight, blooms with red thorns.
The reds, whispered to the wind, loneliness.
Wrinkle stone said, it was the forgotten tears that etched our thoughts.

Once upon a time, loneliness became your favorite with no choice.
Write it in the square house, brand wishes away by light years.
After all, the desolate tree is flourishing because you missed us or raised from our no response ?
Mother! What stupid hopes, looking forward to your tears, drove away my hardwood mold, when I left silently for no reason.
Unfamiliar hug, is it alienated by long absence from distance, or is it my treason ?
Anticipation, a contrast that has never been the truth.

The dry river no longer looks forward to the spring rain.
So, who is who's tangled, hold on to the rush past and my future ?

濱海札記

Finally pull my hand touched your last heartbeat,
the last appeal responded of my tears,
Ugh! life congested punishment.

Seashore variegates

濱海札記

十四行詩|sonnet

春繪旁白

Narrator Spring anecdote

A1 春繪（A1-1）

A1　Spring anecdote（A1-1）

A1　春繪（A1-2）

A1　Spring anecdote（A1-2）

安東尼・賴

春繪旁白

　　2018 春天與太太遊拿波里（那不勒斯），在旅館用早餐，欣賞對面的 egg castle （Castel dell'Ovo）

　　驚覺歲月如梭，想起我們在十年前，淡水漁人碼頭一遊，遇見一位老畫師，繪了一幅素描，當時我有感，寫下春繪。

春繪（淡水記行）

Anthony Lai

Sonnet

Narrator Spring anecdote

At 2018 Spring, with my wife visit Naples.
Breakfast at the hotel and admire the egg castle.
(Castel dell 'Ovo)

I was surprised that the years went by, thinking of been accidental tour Tamsui ten years ago, same dinning in front of sea, and memorized the painter who sketched for her, and later I composed-Spring anecdote-(Tamsui annal)

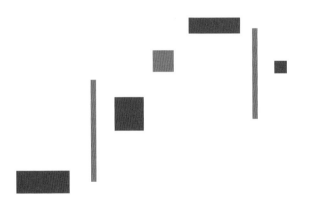

安東尼・賴
十四行詩 A1

春　繪（A1-1）

乍別料峭辭殘冬　左岸櫻花相映紅
頃攬綬衣隨春去　臨滬碧波水漾中
登樓台　臨亭榭　葡萄美酒玉晶杯
銀風撫面　逐帆點點　黑森林咖啡

漁蹤泯沒舨舵遠　碼頭新壨長情橋
麗客如絲織不斷　艇樟盡成賞景船
憶當年　登觀音　嬋媛十九君未識
鰹情何在？而今　鐲鏤結繻參拾載

煙嵐不解韶顏訴　拂耳細語有似無
鬢雲釵頭斜旖旎　楚腰掌中猶纖細
雪肌凝脂暗藏香　疊思憶緬自盈扉
愁笑還憐磯碇處　猶如紋鱗鉤上飛

淺笑中　目流盼　姹紫嫣紅　華爭艷
攝拍……己然萬千詩篇

Anthony Lai

Sonnet A1

Spring anecdote (A1-1)

Last glance of winter chill tells the cherry blossoms on the
left shore, are in red.
Embracing the ribbons in a hurry, go with the spring, while
blue fondle consoles.
Ascend the platform, to the pavilions, toasted crystal seal,
and the grape wine.
Silver wind touches our phiz, dashing the sails and Black-
Forest manual coffee.

No fishman, the craft changed to scenic vessels.
Marina across with new love bridge, traveler nontextured.
Recalling up to Guanyin hill climb, was her 19 years old.
Unknow where you are, but now been married 30 years.

Wind and smoke sages whispers, time passed by.
Am I still young and beauty ? Your skin is still fragrant snow
white.
The gloom hair slanting with memories hairpins are still
enchanting ?

Yes, your thin waist still slender.
Sorrowful and self-pity as fish around reefs, caught away.

Take a smilling picture,
poetries is here.

安東尼 · 賴
十四行詩　A1

春　繪（A1-2）

忽見站前描繪檯　匠師穎清傲群英
前詢摹擬臨素樣　渴得風韻長思量
腆尚座　錠鋏框　鋪紙稿　軸緒線
構勒速筆意輪廓　再定黛眉鎖雙瞳

額飾純醇生百慧　花瓣姝唇擁頰間
炭瑰粗摩捲娉雲　舞瀲飄渺逸垂肩
玉肌霜凝泫瓊瑤　粉頸瑩澤延胸紓
馥陲雙耳羅弦月　嘴角伶笑俏還嗔

Anthony Lai

Sonnet A1

Spring anecdote (A1-2)

Surprised to the painting platform in front of the station
plaza, talented painter looks dexterity special.
Asked for imitate, etching her aspects and frozen this
moment. Sit shy, ingot frame, paper-laying, axis thread.
Sketch contour quick first, then set her eyebrows with eyes
together.

Forehead decorated with pure, rose petals are between the
cheeks.
Thickly charcoal curved and rolled the hair clouds, dancing
ethereal, and hanging upon shoulders.

Glossy skin frost condensed as precious jasper,
pink neck watering, breast wave extension relieves.
Incense ears line dividing as first quarter moon,
smiling come out from the smart mouth nook.

Smear shallow block, release glow white, wipe ridge, double
edges.
In addition to the postfix, sculpted facial frame, darker and
white, signed, spray, solid, cocoon.
Sighed with relief, proud in his works.
Felt the picture is unparalleled in detail, the image gospel as
her.

啟抹塊　擰橡擦　暈澱影　鑑紛溟
除餘補綴　雕顏薄掩　泓黑粉白　署名噴固　繭藏
懍然收筆微嘆息　上端下詳皆得意
像畫緻細無倫比　邐倚韻深魂魄釀

商隱隨遊動記行　淺詞疵賦馨難書
但願春繪遺千歲　淡水右岸凝眸時

To describe incenses details is so hard to fulfill,
only wish this draw can recording the period when sigh at
Tamsui.

Seashore variegates

濱海札記

十四行詩|sonnet

安東尼・賴

詩　b1

阿偉幫媽媽買泡麵（金銀島）

「阿偉——幫媽買泡麵」　高興地從三樓跑下

「錢呢？」「在小皮包裡」「放那？」「下樓——便餐臺——左」

「瓦斯爐對面——置飯鍋櫃第三層——半透明洗菜盆裡——小塑袋裝著」

「小姐——泡麵在那？」「右轉——看置奶櫃——面向它左轉——再左轉」「看到冷凍冰櫃——再右轉——看到酒置格——下四」「如果沒有——再往前看到醬料那一排——往下格找，一定有」

「媽——泡麵來啦！找十元」「給你當零用錢」

寶貝地——用透明小塑盒裝著——置書桌　第四抽屜

最裡面——最私秘的藏

「阿偉——幫老師找資料」　高興地跑上講臺

「資料放那？」「圖書館——大門入——左轉——閱覽室右側梯——樓上右側小門」

「進門左邊——Ｆ區——ＦＰ格第三欄——編號三三七——迷」

阿偉把得到的獎狀——用ＰＥ護套——置書桌第四抽屜——最私秘的藏

濱海札記

Anthony Lai

Poetry b1

Awie's Treasure Land

"<u>Awei</u>, buy instant noodles for mom.", happily ran down from third floor.

" Money ? " "In the small purse." "Where?" "Downstairs, dining table, left side, opposite the gas stove, the third drawer under the rice cooker, the cabinet covered by the translucent vegetable basin, in a small plastic bag."

"Miss, where is the instant noodles ? " "Turn right, look at the milk cabinet, face it and turn left, and turn left again." "See the freezer, turn right again, see the wine grid, fourth level." "If not, go ahead and see the rows of sauces, the bottom grid, must be there." "Mom, the instant noodles are here, dib ten yuan." " Your pocket money."

<u>Awei</u> open his Treasure Land, and put into a small transparent plastic box, placed in the fourth drawer of his desk, the most private storage.

"<u>Awei</u>, find facts for teacher." happily ran up to the podium.

"Where ? " "Library incision, left, reading room right ladder, upstairs right area, section F, column 3 of the FP grid, No. 327, riddle."

<u>Awei</u> puts the certificate of award, with a PE sheath, and put into the fourth drawer of his desk, the most private possession.

"<u>Awei</u>, find love" "Where and how?" "Breeze knows"
"Offer expensive wild rose, electricized hold her hands, and gentle

「阿偉——幫我找愛情」「在那？」「風裡」「怎找？」

「痴痴地——要約——破費地——玫瑰——觸電地——牽手——溫柔地——搭肩」

「緊緊地——攬腰——情深地——凝視——飢渴地——懷抱——尋覓地——輕吻」

「貪婪地——卸衣——瘋狂地——愛撫——肆意地——挑弄——滾燙地——赤裸」「而後用舌挑開緊閉的雙唇——吮吸著舌根——接生初誕的——愛情」

阿偉寫了一首詩——置書桌第四抽屜藍皮本夾裡——最私秘的藏

「阿偉——幫阿公找牌位」「埋那？」「地裡」

「怎麼找？」

「午時——去那排血紅色公寓後山——拿刀——砍除那人間久遠的荒煙蔓草」

「尋到——精卵印下的嘆息足跡——牽著——祖先不足為人道的豐功偉業」

「看著——滿地枯骨棄棺破甕 乏人禮拜的絕子絕孫」

「飛著——魂魄穿出太陽系 到銀河中心黑洞的 物質奔流裡——找到——逝去」

「是遺失的『空』，或者是滿足的『恆』」

「上香給 接絃永續不斷的——你的根——你的祖」

阿偉留了一束殘香——紅色香袋奉著——置書桌第四抽屜族譜內——最私祕的藏

stand on her shoulder" "A tight waist hold, deeply stared, hungry clasped, seek lips, kiss lightly."

"Unloading greedily, caress frantically, wantonly tease, and hotly naked, then use tongue to open her lips, sucking the core, awake the first birth of love."

Awei wrote poems on blue paper, envelop in the fourth drawer of his desk as the amplest bosom.

"Awei, try to find grandpa's memorial tablet? " "In the ground? " "How?"

"At noon, go to the mountain behind that row of blood-red apartments, take a sword, slash time spooky weed of ancestor."

"Find sights of sperm in the uterus, holding the ancestors' trivial great deeds."

"Looking at land full of withered bones, abandoning coffins and breaking urns, those have no descendant to worship."

"Teleport, your soul out of solar system into the black hole at the center of the galaxy, look at their passing moment."

"They were missing into emptiness or fulfilled perpetually."

"Salute, spark the strings to be continuous your roots and your ancestors."

Awei left a bunch of residual incense put in a red sachet, holding in the fourth drawer of his desk as the most private legacy.

"Awei, redeem yourself." "Where?" "In oblivion."

"Take spaceship Discovery through the wormhole of the parallel universe, perforates subspace of Eris, back to memories, and create a Big Ban by yourself."

「阿偉──幫自己找回失落」「在那？」「在遺忘裡」「那找？」

「搭時光公車──經平行宇宙的蟲洞──穿過空魁的　亞空間──回到回憶的大霹靂奇點」

「在爆炸後的數十億分之一秒裡──鑽入深藍──在深藍宇宙裡邊緣──找到『恨痛』銀河」

「在恨的銀河找到『怒星系』──在痛的銀河找到『麻木星系』──兩星系連結的座點」

「有顆灰白的七等星叫──嘆息──外層──傲慢的鑽石結晶体包圍」

「穿過並躍入偏見的熔岩──你就會看到它的核心叫『愚蠢』」

「存若干隱形儲存室──唯有半透明的叫『遺忘』」

「裡面放著你久遠的書桌第四個抽屜」

阿偉把新書桌第四抽屜拿掉──寶貝地──把新尋到的舊抽屜放好──最私秘的藏

「小小阿偉──幫阿嬤買泡麵」「錢呢？」「在阿公的口袋裡」

"In one billionth of a second after the explosion, drilling into the deep blue, in the dark maters, find the hate and pain galaxy."

"Find 'Anger' in the nebula of hate and find 'Numbness' in the cluster of pain, at the twist point, there is a gray-white star of seventh magnitude called 'Sigh'

outer layer surrounded by arrogant diamond crystals."

"Go through and jump into the lava of prejudice, you will see that moronic core."

"There are some dormant storage rooms, only the translucent one is called 'forgotten', hides the fourth drawer of your old desk"

Awei takes out the fourth drawer of new desk, put the old drawer which newly found, as the newest Treasure Land in his life.

"Awei junior, help Grandma buy instant noodles." "Where's the money?" "In Grandpa's pocket"

妹の姿（給玥寧）

眼中的地中海　波斯深藍

要向你　展示　神秘的未來

白鴿子和小袋鼠　在　風中跳舞

伸展手指　寫沒有字母的　物語

我們都是她的　車　供呼喚

只有哥哥不是

哥哥稱她　妹之姿

金色夏日　馬尾　海市蜃樓

調皮地　撒上　高音　外星語

我想讓你　發動　隨風

卻　常仿媽媽　清潔動作

表示　即將成長

她會用眼神 Q 你　在吃飯　桌上

因為　誰也不會　想吻　臉上　油麵